This book belongs to:

....

First published 1987 by Walker Books Ltd
87 Vauxhall Walk, London SE11 5HJ

This edition published 1991. © 1987 Jill Murphy

Printed and bound in
Hong Kong by Imago

British Library Cataloguing in Publication Data
Murphy, Jill
All in one piece.
I. Title
823'.914 [J] PZ7
ISBN 0-7445-2116-5

All in One Piece
Jill Murphy

WALKER BOOKS
LONDON

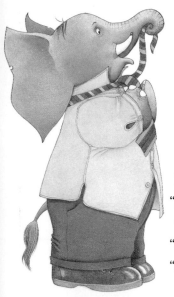

Mr Large was getting ready for work.
"Don't forget the office dinner-dance
   tonight, dear," he said.
"Of course I won't," said Mrs Large.
"I've been thinking about it all year."

"Are children allowed at the dinner-dance?"
 asked Lester.
"No," said Mrs Large. "It'll be too late
 for little ones."
"What about the baby?" asked Luke.
"Granny is coming to take care of everyone,"
 said Mrs Large, "so there's no need to worry."

Granny arrived at tea time. The children
were already bathed and in their nightclothes.
Granny gave them some painting to do while
she tidied up and Mr and Mrs Large went
upstairs to get ready.

Luke sneaked into the bathroom while
Mr Large was shaving.
"Will I have to shave when I grow up?"
he asked, patting foam onto his trunk.
"Go away," said Mr Large. "I don't want
you ruining my best trousers!"

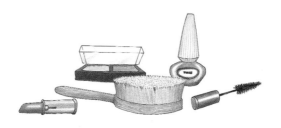

The baby crept into the bedroom where
Mrs Large was putting on her make-up.
Mrs Large didn't notice until it was too late.

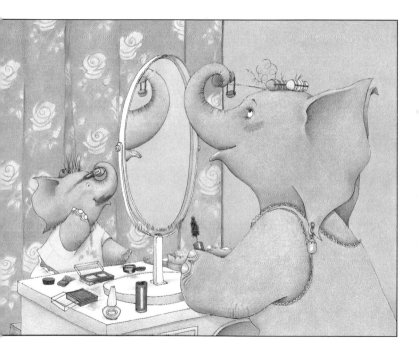

"Look!" said the baby. "Pretty!"
"Don't move," said Mrs Large. "Don't
  touch *anything*!"
Outside on the landing, things were
even worse. Laura was clopping about in
her mother's best shoes and beads and
Lester and Luke were seeing how many
toys they could cram into her new tights.

"Downstairs at *once*!" bellowed Mrs Large.
"Can't I have just one night in the whole year
to myself? One night when I am not covered in
jam and poster-paint? One night when I can put
on my new dress and walk through the front
door all in one piece?"

The children went downstairs to Granny.
Mr Large followed soon after, very smart
in his best suit. At last, Mrs Large
appeared in the doorway.
"How do I look?" she asked.

"Pretty, Mummy!" gasped the children.

"What a smasher!" said Mr Large.

"You look like a film star, dear,"
 said Granny.

"Hands off!" said Mrs Large to the
 paint-smeared children.

Mr and Mrs Large got ready to leave.

"Goodbye everyone," they said. "Be good now."

The baby began to cry.

"Just go," said Granny, picking her up.

"She'll stop as soon as you've left. Have a
lovely time."

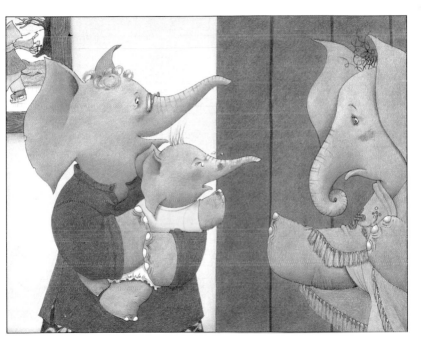

"We've escaped," said Mr Large with a smile,
    closing the front door behind them.
"All in one piece," said Mrs Large, "and
    not a smear of paint between us."
"Actually," said Mr Large gallantly, "you'd
    look wonderful to me, even if you were
    covered in paint."

Which was perfectly true…
and just as well really!